The Thing at the Foot of the Bed

AND OTHER SCARY TALES

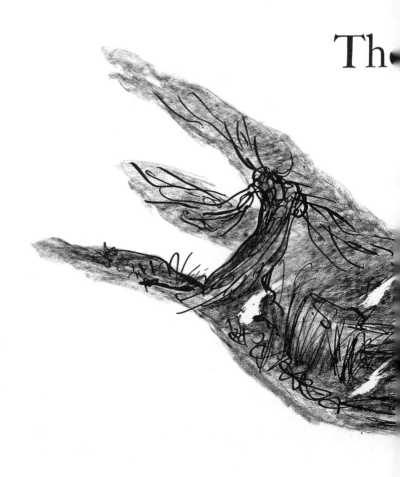

Th

By the same author

Noodles, Nitwits, and
Numskulls

Thing at the Foot of the Bed

AND OTHER SCARY TALES

By *Maria Leach*

ILLUSTRATED BY *Kurt Werth*

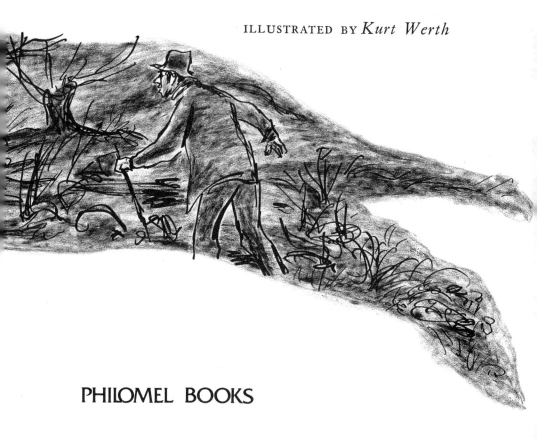

PHILOMEL BOOKS

Copyright © 1959 by Maria Leach
Published by Philomel Books
a division of The Putnam Publishing Group
200 Madison Avenue, New York, NY 10016
Library of Congress Cataloging in Publication Data
Leach, Maria.
The thing at the foot of the bed, and other scary tales.
Reprint. Originally published: Cleveland: World, 1959.
Bibliography: p. 1 2 5
Summary: A collection of ghost stories originating
in folk tales told the world over.
1. Tales. 2. Ghost stories. [1. Folklore. 2. Ghosts—Fiction]
I. Werth, Kurth, ill. II. Title.
PZ8.1.L36Th 1982 398'.47 81-22746
ISBN 0-399-61207-6 (lib. bdg.) AACR2

Contents

What did one little ghost say to the other little ghost?

Do you believe in people?

Some People Say

SOME people say there are no such things as ghosts because they have never seen one. *Seeing is believing,* they say. And some people say there are so such things as ghosts because they *have* seen them. And *seeing is believing,* they say.

But even the ones who do not believe in ghosts are afraid of them! They *like* being afraid of them, for there is something in the human mind that loves to scare itself to death! But did you ever notice that the scariest stories are usually the funniest? The terrible thing turns out to be a flapping nightshirt or a pet monkey promenading in a tablecloth. Or else it is the storyteller himself who scares you, makes you scream or jump—not a ghost at all.

What *is* a ghost? It is not always an invisible spirit, because often you may meet up with someone who looks and talks and acts just like any real person, and you never find out it was a ghost until it vanishes or reveals its identity in some way.

Sweet William was one of these. He had a hard time convincing sweet Margret that he was "no earthly man" and could not go to the church and be married. The ghostly hitchhiker is another. The motorist who picks up the pretty girl in the road late at night is always stunned to learn that she is dead.

9

Other ghosts in this book who resemble the living and fool those whom they encounter are the guitar player in one of the ghost-race stories, the men whose teeth were "as long as this," the young dead mother who bought milk for her living baby, the phantom sailors who climbed aboard the ship which had run them down, and Aunt Tilly, who momentarily came to the family party which her illness and death had prevented her attending.

A ghost is usually believed to be the soul of someone who is dead, and people call them ghosts, phantoms, specters, spooks, or haunts. Another word is *revenant*, which means "returner."

They return for all kinds of reasons. They return to aid, comfort, advise, reward, or warn the living or to save them from some terrible danger.

There is a legend that whenever England is in danger, the drum of Sir Francis Drake will be heard through the land to give warning. But this is more than a legend in England, for Drake's drum was heard in the night in many a small coastal town before World War I and again before World War II.

It is told that during World War I when the Germans were approaching Paris they were halted by the sudden appearance of a luminous figure in the road with a flaming sword and a dark army behind her. It was Joan of Arc who saved Paris in World War I, they say.

There is another story that during World War II in Occupied France the Germans noticed a quiet nun who would go through the hospitals giving special aid to the French wounded. She was an "unauthorized" worker, but whenever they tried to stop or question her she somehow always evaded them. Finally they went to the convent to make a search; but they did not find the one they were after. Suddenly one of the men recognized her picture on the wall. It was Joan of Arc.

Sometimes ghosts return to stop the grieving of those who weep for them, to re-enact some tragedy in their own lives over and over, to pay a debt or to reward the one who does so for them, to ask or give forgiveness.

Sometimes a ghost stands guard over buried treasure for hundreds of years until it finds the *right one* to give it to. Or sometimes ghosts wander around just because they are uneasy in their graves, like Anne Boleyn, who is seen every year on the date of her execution walking through the Tower of London carrying her head in the crook of her arm.

And sometimes ghosts return to punish some crime, and of course to reveal murder and bring murderers to justice. These ghosts, the avenging ghosts, are no doubt the reason why people fear all ghosts, the reason why just the idea of ghosts raises gooseflesh on the skin and terror in the mind. But unless you have really harmed someone who is dead, you have nothing to fear from any ghost you may see or hear or meet.

I once knew a little boy who did not like ghost stories "because they are always so sad." And this is often true (as the tales called *Real Ones* in this book show). But very few people stop to realize it.

Usually a ghost is just some poor harmless soul, unhappy and lonely and wandering about, looking for someone with enough understanding and kindness to speak to it or do it some little favor.

Funny Ones

Six little ghostses
Sittin' on postses
Eatin' buttered toastses

The Thing at the Foot of the Bed

ONCE there was a man and they dared him to sleep all night in a haunted house.

"All right," he said. He wasn't scared of anything. He'd sleep there. No such thing as ghosts, anyway.

So he went into the house and looked around. Everything looked all right. So he went upstairs. Everything looked all right. So he went to bed.

He lay there in bed a while and listened. He didn't hear anything. So he went to sleep. It was a warm night, so he had no covers but a sheet.

The man slept a while, and then suddenly he woke up. He listened. He didn't hear anything.

The moon was shining bright through the open window. So—very carefully—very quietly—he looked around. And he saw, down at the foot of the bed, two shiny eyes staring right at him. They looked something like this:

They didn't even blink.

Was that a head—a face?

The man thought he could make out the top of a flat crooked head.

He *was* scared.

He didn't dare move.

But softly, very softly, he slid his hand up under the pillow and pulled out the revolver he'd brought with him.

He aimed at the thing, right between the eyes. He was so scared, though, that his hand trembled and wiggled and shook, and . . .

(S C R E A M)

Here the teller of the tale gives a terrifying scream—and is then silent. Finally, when someone says, "What was it?" he explains, "The poor scared fool shot off his own big toe." (His feet were sticking out below the sheet, and the moonlight shining on the nails of his big toes looked like two ghostly eyes.)

Here We Go!

ONCE there was a rich farmer who had a fine farm, fine horses and cattle, a fine big house, and a fine wife and several children. He was a very happy man—happy, that is, except for one thing. There was a boggart in the house.

Boggart is a north-of-England word for a kind of trick-playing spirit which takes up its abode in people's houses and barns. Some say it is a ghost, and some say it is just a mischief-maker. It never really hurts anyone, but it can play a lot of painful practical jokes.

This farmer and his wife had a boggart. It used to walk around in the house at night and pull the covers off of people. It used to knock on the door and when the sleepy farmer got up and went downstairs to open it, there would be nobody there.

It used to fall downstairs in the dark, making an awful racket, and when the wife ran into the hall, fearing it was one of the children, all the children would be safely asleep in bed.

Sometimes it would just tap, tap, tap in the night on the lid of the linen chest. Sometimes it would roll a heavy ball across the floor, time and again, so no one could sleep, or let it go bump-bumping down the stairs. One night it threw all the pots and pans down the cellar stairs. That was a clatter!

Once in a while the boggart would pitch in and help the family. It would wash the dishes when the farmer's wife wasn't looking; or sometimes it would churn the butter or collect the eggs. It would feed and water the cows and horses. But more often than not it would tie knots in their tails or let them loose in the night so the farmer had to go looking for them. Once it broke all the cups and saucers.

One of its favorite tricks was to blow all the smoke back *down* the chimney whenever anyone tried to light a fire. Or it would blow out the match just when someone was trying to make a light.

At last the farmer and his wife got tired of all this. They could put up with a prank now and then. But this boggart was so annoying and troublesome that something had to be done.

So they decided to move. They decided to move to a new house on a big farm far away where there would be no boggarts.

The man and his wife and children packed up all their belongings and piled them high on the big wagon.

Just as they were about to drive off, a neighbor came by and said, "Oh, are you moving?"

"Yes," said the man. He explained that the boggart's tricks had at last become unbearable. They could not stand their boggart any longer, so they were moving.

So the neighbor wished them luck, and they drove off. Then from the top of the load they heard a little voice say happily, "Well, here we go! We're off!"

Ghost Race

1. The Guitar Player

ONCE there was a man who played the guitar in the streets of Paramaribo in Surinam (Dutch Guiana).

He played all day and as late into the night as people would listen and give him a little money. Sometimes he was paid to come into their houses and play for parties.

He was a very fine player.

One night very late he was going home from a party and was playing the guitar softly to himself as he went along.

He met a man in the road and the man said, "Will you let me play it?"

So he said, "Sure!" and handed the guitar to the stranger.

The stranger played marvelously. His playing was more wonderful than any the man had ever heard in his life.

"Man! *That's* how to play the guitar!" he said.

"Well—" said the other modestly, "that used to be my work when I was living."

"Gosh! Are you dead?" And the man began to run.

"Here! You forgot your guitar!"

The other ran after him. "Here's your guitar!" he yelled.

"Keep it!" the man yelled back.

But the other caught up with him. "Here's your guitar," he said.

"Keep it!" And the man ran faster than ever.

At last he got home and fell into bed. And when he opened the door in the morning, there was his guitar on the doorstep.

2. Never Mind Them Watermelons

ONCE there was a man who said he didn't believe in ghosts, didn't believe in haunts, didn't believe in haunted houses. Another man said he'd give him a whole wagonload of watermelons if he would spend the night in a certain old empty house down the road.

The man said, sure, he'd sleep there, so he picked up his matches and tobacco and set out. He went in the house and lighted his pipe. He sat down in a chair and started to read the paper.

Pretty soon something sat down beside him and said, "Ain't nobody here but you and me?"

"Ain't gonna be nobody but you in a minute," said the man. So he jumped out the window and started to run. He ran pretty fast, overtook two rabbits going the same way. Pretty soon something caught up with him and said, "Well, you makin' pretty good speed."

"Oh, I can run faster than this," said the man—and did.

When he passed the man who gave him the dare, he said, "Never mind about them watermelons."

From *The Rainbow Book of American Folk Tales and Legends* by Maria Leach, The World Publishing Company, 1958. By permission of the publishers.

Wait Till Martin Comes

THAT big house down the road was haunted. Nobody could live in it.

The door was never locked. But nobody ever went in. Nobody would even spend a night in it. Several people had tried but came running out pretty fast.

One night a man was going along that road on his way to the next village. He noticed that the sky was blackening. No moon. No stars. Big storm coming for sure.

He had a long way to go. He knew he couldn't get home before it poured.

So he decided to take shelter in that empty house by the road.

He had heard it was haunted. But shucks! Who believed in ghosts? No such thing.

So he went in. He built himself a nice fire on the big hearth, pulled up a chair, and sat down to read a book.

He could hear the rain beating on the windows. Lightning flashed. The thunder cracked around the old building.

But he sat there reading.

Next time he looked up there was a little gray cat sitting on the hearth.

That was all right, he thought. Cozy.

He went on reading. The rain went on raining.

Pretty soon he heard the door creak and a big black cat came sauntering in.

The first cat looked up.

"What we goin' to do with him?"

"Wait till Martin comes," said the other.

The man went right on reading.

Pretty soon he heard the door creak and another great big black cat, as big as a dog, came in.

"What we goin' to do with him?" said the first cat.

"Wait till Martin comes."

The man was awful scared by this time, but he kept looking in the book, pretending to be reading.

Pretty soon he heard the door creak and a great big black cat, as big as a calf, came in.

He stared at the man. "Shall we do it now?" he said.

"Wait till Martin comes," said the others.

The man just leaped out of that chair, and out the window, and down the road.

"Tell Martin I couldn't wait!" he said.

Big Fraid and Little Fraid

ONCE there was a little boy who was not afraid of anything. He used to go out on errands and come home long after dark.

His father didn't like this and tried everything to make him come home on time. But the boy paid no attention.

"Aren't you afraid?" the father said.

"What is a fraid?" said the boy. "I never saw a fraid."

"You will!" said the father.

He used to send the little boy to bring home the cows in the evening. And the boy would always come in late, singing in the road in the dark.

So the man decided to put a stop to it.

One night he got a big white sheet and put it over his head and went down to the gate to wait for the boy.

Now this man had a pet monkey who used to follow him around. When the monkey saw the man put the sheet over his head, he grabbed a little white cloth off a little table and put it over his own head and followed the man out of the house.

The man did not know the monkey was following.

The man went and hid behind the big white gatepost. And
when the monkey saw that, he hid behind the other gatepost.

It got late; it got dark. And soon the boy came along home.

He saw the big white shape by the gatepost.

"Oh! That must be a fraid," he said. But he was not frightened.

"Oh! There's another fraid!" he said.

So the man thought if there was *another* one, there must be
a real one there!

He looked. And he saw a little white figure bouncing up and
down by the other gatepost.

He was scared to death and lit out for the house with his white
sheet flapping behind him. When the monkey saw his master
run, he ran after him.

"Look at Big Fraid running away from Little Fraid!" said
the boy.

The Lucky Man

ONCE there was a man lying in bed asleep. And he woke up. He heard something flapping.

He got up. He walked softly to the window.

And he saw it.

It was white—flapping in the moonlight. It was under a tree. It would flap its arms out in the moonlight and then slip back into the shadow of the tree.

"It's a ghost," thought the man. "I'll fix him before he gets into the house."

Very stealthily he took his gun down off the wall where he hung it at night. And he shot holes in the flapping thing, one after another. But it went on flapping.

At last the man went back to bed. If he hadn't killed it, at least he had scared it, he thought, for it stayed in the shadow of the tree and came no nearer.

In the morning the man got up and went downstairs. His wife was already in the kitchen.

"You fool!" she said. "Shooting your clean nightshirt full of holes!" (She had washed it the day before and hung it in the tree to dry.)

"My nightshirt!" said the man. "Gosh! Lucky I wasn't in it!"

30

Scary Ones

The Golden Arm

ONCE there was a man had a woman for a wife named Elvira, and this woman had a golden arm. She was awful proud of it. It was solid shining gold from the shoulder clear down to the nail of her little finger. She liked it even better than the real one.

Every night when she went to bed she used to say to her husband, "If I die first, promise to bury me with my golden arm."

"Yes, Elviry, I promise," the man would say, night after night after night.

Well, it happened that the woman got sick and died. The man buried her and her golden arm along with her, just as he had promised.

But after a while he began to think about it. He began to think about what he could do with all that gold. It seemed a shame for it just to lie there in the ground. He began to *want* the golden arm. And the more he thought about it, the more he wanted it.

So one dark night in the middle of the night he decided to

33

go get it. He put on his long dark coat and he lighted his lantern and he went trudging through the cold dark lanes till he came to the graveyard. And he dug up Elvira and took the golden arm.

He tucked it under his long coat and started back home. On the way home it started to rain, hail, snow, and blow. But he didn't think anything of that. He got home all right.

When he got home he didn't know where to hide the golden arm, so he pushed it under the covers of the bed. Then he jumped into bed himself and shivered and shook. He couldn't get warm because the golden arm was cold as ice.

And the wind rose and he heard a voice wailing

W-H-E-E-R-E'-S M-Y G-O-O-L-D-E-N A-A-A-R-M?

The man pulled the covers up over his head so he wouldn't hear it. But he heard it just the same.

He heard it coming down the road. It was crying in the road

W-H-E-E-R-E'-S M-Y-Y

and on the porch

G-O-O-L-D-E-N

and at the door

A-A-A-R-M?

And the wind howled over the top of the door

W-H-E-E-R-E'-S M-Y G-O-L-D-E-N A-A-R-M?

The man shivered and shook under the covers. Then he peeked out.

And he saw it.
　　It was by the bed.
　　　　And—it pounced

YOU'VE GOT IT!

· · ·

This is one of the most famous scary stories told. It is said to have been told around every Boy and Girl Scout campfire ever kindled.

This is the story Mark Twain used to tell to scare whole audiences. And he explained that it is the timing of the pause just before the pounce that makes for success or failure in the telling. If you get the pause just right, he said, someone in the audience will surely scream!

I have told the story here as well as I can remember of the way it was told to me in Shelburne County, Nova Scotia. It is a windy-night story, they say. Whenever the east wind howls loud and lonesome over a door at night, someone says, "Elvira wants her golden arm."

The Dare

ONCE there was a bunch of youngsters sitting in front of a fire telling ghost stories and trying to scare each other.

There had been a funeral in the village that day. An old man had been buried that afternoon, an old man noted for his crankiness and cussing. The boys had used to torment him, just to hear him rage in helpless fury.

One of the group said if anyone walked on that old man's grave at midnight, he would reach up and grab him.

"Oh, rot! No such thing!" said a boy named Jim.

"Well, I dare you!" said another.

"I dare you!"

"I dare you!"

They all joined in.

"All right!" said the bragging one. "I don't believe in ghosts. I'll go do it."

"I dare you!"

"I'll do it, and I'll stick my jackknife in the grave! And you can all go see it in the morning."

So the party broke up.

When midnight came, the boy named Jim started for the graveyard. It was awful quiet. The tombstones made long shadows in the moonlight. He was pretty scared. But he could not back out now, so he went on.

Could the old geezer reach up and grab him? he wondered. He wished he had not been so smart and taken on this dare.

But he went on.

He came to the grave. He took out his jackknife and opened it. He knelt down and jabbed it blindly into the mound over the grave.

Then he started to get up and run home. But he could not move! Something *had* grabbed him. He could not budge from the grave.

The next day was a school day and Jim was absent from his classes.

The boys all wondered where he was. And at noontime several of them decided to go to the graveyard and see if Jim had left his jackknife sticking in the grave.

When they got there they found Jim lying in a little heap on the new-made mound.

In his haste and panic he had thrust the knife through his own coattails. He had pinned himself to the old man's grave, and had died of fright.

I'm in the Room!

ONCE there was a young woman named Rosie, who lived in a small Louisiana town. She could see ghosts.

She didn't really *like* seeing them. The very first time she saw one she was awful scared. But after a while she got used to it.

The first time Rosie ever saw a ghost she was lying in bed all alone. She was just about to go to sleep, when suddenly she opened her eyes and there was a ghost.

It was tall and white.

It said, "Rosie, I'm in the room."

She was scared.

"I'm standing by the bed," it said.

She covered up her head.

"I'm pulling down the quilt!" it said. And it was.

Rosie trembled and shook.

"I'm getting in the bed!" it said. Rosie was so scared she couldn't speak.

"I—GOT YOU!"

And it grabbed her.

Then Rosie screamed.

Then she looked again and there wasn't any ghost there at all.

No Head

ONE DAY when a certain man was plowing his field he looked up and saw a man without a head walking to meet him.

He was too scared to speak, so he just looked down and went on plowing. When he dared look back, old No Head had disappeared.

"Next time I won't be scared," the man thought.

The next day when the man was plowing he looked up and saw No Head again walking to meet him.

He was scareder than ever. He couldn't say a word—just went on plowing.

After a while he looked back and old No Head had vanished.

"Next time I *won't* be scared," he thought.

The next day it happened again. The man was plowing his field, and he looked up and saw the headless man walking to meet him.

He was just as scared as ever, but he screwed up his courage and said, "Hello, Mr. No Head. What do you want?"

"Lucky thing you spoke at last!" said old No Head, "or I would have knocked your head off too, this time!"

(Of course, everyone knows that ghosts can't speak until they are spoken to.)

"Go dig under that tree," said No Head. "There's money there. And give the boss half!"

So the man started to dig under the tree. Soon the shovel hit silver money and he knew old No Head was right.

Just then the boss came driving past the field in his wagon.

"Hey, boss. Come dig!" the man yelled.

And he told the boss about old No Head and what he had said.

"Nonsense!" said the boss, and started to drive on.

But—*the horses wouldn't budge!*

"Giddap!" said the boss.

But the horses stomped and rared and stayed right in the same place.

"That's funny!" said the boss.

42

(Of course, everyone knows that horses won't go ahead if there's a ghost in the road.)

So he got down from the wagon and started to help the man dig.

They found a big bag of money. The bag was rotted away and the two shovels made a lovely clink against the coins.

After that the two men were both rich.

As Long As This?

Once there was a man going home along a dark road at night. And he met a man.

The man spoke to him and said, "Can I light my cigarette? I have no match."

"Sure! Light it on my cigarette!"

He reached out his cigarette to the other and then the man grinned and showed his teeth. They were as long as this!

The man ran. He ran and ran. Soon he met another man, who said, "Why are you running?"

"Oh, my friend! I just met a man whose teeth were as long as this!" And he showed him how long.

And the new man said, "Were they as long as this?" and then he grinned. This one's teeth were as long as this!

So the man knew he had met up with a *yorka*. (*Yorka* is the Surinam Negro word for ghost.) He was scared to death. He ran and ran.

Soon he met another man in the road. Anyway, it *looked* like another man. And this one said, "My poor fellow! Why do you run?"

"Oh!" said the man. "I met a man back there in the road with teeth as long as this!" And he showed him how long.

"But not as long as this!" said the stranger. He grinned then, and his teeth were as long as this!

The man ran. He ran and ran and never stopped till he was home in bed.

The Legs

ONCE there was a poor young boy who was an orphan and had no place to live. There were plenty of rich people in that town; but nobody said, "Come and live with us," so he used to sleep out under trees or in barns with the warm cows and horses.

But one cold day an old man told the boy he could have that big house on the hill if he would stay in it overnight.

"All right," said the boy.

"It's haunted," said the man.

"All right," said the boy.

So he went up the hill to the house. He opened the door and went in. Everything looked all right. There was even a big warm fire already burning on the hearth. So he just set to and started to cook his supper.

Just as he was sitting down on a stool by the fire to eat, he heard a scrabbling in the chimney.

A voice cried out, "I'm going to drop it!"

"All right," said the boy, "but not in my soup!" And he hitched over a little to be out of the way.

And a great big, ugly, hairy bare leg fell down the chimney.

The boy shoved it to one side with his foot so it wouldn't get scorched in the fire.

It was good soup he was eating. He certainly did enjoy it. He was just starting on the second bowl when the voice said, "I'm going to drop it!"

"All right," said the boy, "but not in my soup!" And he gave the stool another hitch to get out of the way.

Down came another great ugly, hairy bare leg. It would have been uglier than the first one except it was just like it. The boy shoved it over alongside the other one.

"Have some soup?" he said. But the two legs just lay there.

Then as soon as the boy finished his soup and washed the bowl, those two legs jumped up and grabbed him and dragged him under the house.

He was just beginning to get scared when they began to point at a big flat stone.

So the boy turned the stone over and there was a big chest full of money. After that he lived in the house and was richer than anybody.

Talk

ONCE there was a man who wasn't scared of skeletons or old bones or ghosts or haunts or anything. He never said there *weren't* any. He just wasn't scared of them. That's all.

He would even go walking into a graveyard at night and say, "Rise up, bloody bones! Rise up and shake!"

And the poor tired old bones would pull themselves together and rise up like skeletons and shake in the wind.

The man used to do this every night because it made him feel big and proud.

One night he was walking along the road and stumbled on an old skull. So he kicked it. He kicked it along in front of him as he walked, having fun, seeing how far it would go. And he said, "Rise up, old bone! Rise up and shake!"

But the old skull just lay still in the road and grinned at him. So he left it there and went along toward home. But soon he heard a voice behind him, so he looked back.

There lay the skull in the road, grinning, and it said, "My big mouth brought me here, and yours will do the same!"

So the man went along into the town and told everybody that there was an old white skull bone back there in the road *that talked!* Of course, nobody believed it.

"Well, come with me and I'll show you," he said.

Nobody wanted to go much, but the man said, "Well, come on. And if the old skull don't talk, you can cut my head off right there!"

So the people went along, sure it was all a fake, but ready to take the bet. Finally they came to the skull lying in the road.

The man gave it a kick. But the skull never said a word.

He kicked it again. But the skull never said a word.

He gave it another big kick. But the skull never said a word.

One of the villagers began to sharpen his big knife.

The man gave the skull another desperate kick. "Say something!" he cried.

But the old skull just rolled over sideways—and grinned. It never said a word.

The people were pretty mad, being fooled like that and dragged all that long way in the middle of the night. So they cut off the man's head to square the bet, and went home.

Then the old dry skull grinned at the new bloody one.

"I told you so!" it said.

Dark, Dark, Dark

THE night was dark, dark, dark. I was walking along a dark, dark road and I came to a dark, dark house. I knocked on the dark, dark door.

NOBODY ANSWERED

So I went in through the dark, dark door into a dark, dark hall. "Hello!" I said.

NOBODY ANSWERED

So I went up the dark, dark stairs and I went into a dark, dark room. Over in the dark, dark corner I saw a dark, dark chest. So I opened it—and out jumped—a dark, dark

GHOST

· · · ·

The whole point of this story is in the telling. It can be very dramatic. I first heard it as a child one summer in Yarmouth County, Nova Scotia, when I was allowed to visit a little girl about my own age and stay overnight. She told it to me in the dark, and with the dramatic ending, leaped up standing on the foot of the bed: a miniature ghost herself in the dark, dark room. I have never heard it anywhere else, but perhaps it is told in many places.

You try it!

Real Ones

He beats his fists
Against the posts
And still insists
He sees six ghosts

Sweet William's Ghost

THERE came a ghost to Margret's door,
  With many a grievous groan,
And ay he tirled at the pin,*
But answer made she none.

"Is that my father Philip?
Or is't my brother John?
Or is't my true-love Willy
From Scotland new come home?"

"T'is not thy father Philip,
Nor yet thy brother John.
But t'is thy true-love Willy
From Scotland new come home.

"O sweet Margret, dear Margret,
I pray thee speak to me!
Give me my faith and troth, Margret,
As I gave it to thee."

---

*tirled at the pin, rattled at the latch

"Thy faith and troth thou's never get,
Nor yet will I thee lend
Till that thou come within my bower
And kiss my cheek and chin."

"If I should come within thy bower—
I am no earthly man—
And should I kiss those rosy lips,
Thy days will not be lang.

"O, sweet Margret, dear Margret,
I pray thee speak to me!
Give me my faith and troth, Margret,
As I gave it to thee."

"Thy faith and troth thou's never get,
Nor yet will I thee lend,
Till you take me to yon church
And wed me with a ring."

"My bones are buried in a churchyard
Afar beyond the sea.
And it is but my ghost, Margret,
That's speaking now to thee."

She stretchèd out her lily-white hand,
And, for to do her best,
Said, "There's your faith and troth, Willy,
God send your soul good rest."

Now she has kilted her robes of green
A piece below the knee,
And all the live-lang winter night
The dead corp followed she.

"Is there any room at your head, Willy?
Or any room at your feet?
Or any room at your side, Willy,
Wherein I may creep?"

"There's no room at my head, Margret,
There's no room at my feet.
There's no room at my side, Margret,
My coffin's made so meet."†

Then up and crew the red, red cock,
And up then crew the gray.
"T'is time, t'is time, my dear Margret,
That you were going away."

No more the ghost to Margret said,
But, with a grievous groan,
He vanished in a cloud of mist
And left her all alone.

"O stay, my only true-love, stay!"
The constant Margret cried.
Wan grew her cheeks, she closed her eyes,
Stretched her soft limbs, and died.

Scottish Border ballad

---

†*meet*, close-fitting, fitting exactly

Milk Bottles

THIS happened many years ago in a small country village in Alabama.

One day the storekeeper looked up and saw a pale young woman in a gray dress standing at the counter.

"What can I do for you, ma'am?" he said.

She did not answer, but pointed to a bottle of milk. The storekeeper handed it to her, and without a word she walked quickly out of the store and down the main street of the town.

The next day she came back.

"What will you have today, ma'am?" the storekeeper asked.

The young woman in gray pointed to a bottle of milk.

Again the storekeeper handed it to her. And once again the woman took the milk and hurried away without saying a word.

That night the storekeeper told his neighbors about the strange young woman in gray with the sad, pale face who came every day for milk and walked away without thanks or payment, in silence.

So the next day when the woman in gray appeared and again walked away with the milk without speaking, two or three of the villagers followed her.

She walked swiftly down the main street of the town. The men were amazed that they almost had to run to keep sight of her.

She passed the school; she passed the church; she kept right on through the little town up the hill to the graveyard.

She passed swiftly in among the graves and stones and trees, seemed to stop for a minute—and then was gone.

The followers stood quietly beside the grave where the slender gray figure had seemed to pause. It was the new-made grave of a young mother and her baby daughter who had died three days ago of a fever. In fact, she had died just one day before she first came into the store for milk.

It all seemed so strange and mysterious that the villagers thought they ought to investigate. So they came back with shovels and soon unearthed the young mother's coffin.

Then, while they were moving the coffin, they heard—or thought they heard—a tiny muffled wail.

They listened.

They heard it again—the feeble little cry of a baby.

Quickly they opened the coffin.

Yes. Here was the frail young mother in gray who had come for the milk. And in her arms lay a baby girl—ill and weak, but *alive*.

Beside her lay the empty milk bottles.

One of the men took the baby home to his wife, and the little life was saved.

No one ever saw the young mother in gray again. She had accomplished her task. She had saved her baby girl.

Now she could rest.

The Head

ONCE there were two friends who were very fond of each other; but like all friends they quarreled a little now and then.

Usually the quarrel was over some bit of foolishness. But one day they had a real quarrel. This, too, was a foolish quarrel, as most quarrels are, but the two young men got madder and madder and the quarrel turned into a fight.

They were so mad they pulled out their knives, and that fight ended with one of them slashing off the head of the other.

The one who did it ran and ran until he was far from the city. The police searched everywhere, but they never found him. At last they gave up.

Years went by: one year, two years, five years, six . . . eight . . . ten.

At last, at the end of ten years the murderer thought it would be safe to go home. He did not think anyone would remember or recognize him. And for many weeks he lived alone in a little house, working at whatever jobs came his way.

One day as he was passing through the market he saw a calf's head for sale. He dearly loved a good dish of calf's head, so he stopped and bought it. Then as he was walking home, thinking how good it would be, a policeman stopped him and said, "What is that?"

So the man explained that he had just bought a calf's head to have for his supper.

"Awful bloody calf's head!" said the policeman.

"Oh, it's a fresh one," said the man.

"Let's see it!"

So the man opened the bag and pulled out—not a calf's head at all—but the head of his dead friend. It was dripping with blood, as if it had just been cut off! It had been trickling down behind him, leaving a little stream of blood all the way as he walked along!

So of course they knew that he was the murderer, and they took him and hanged him by the neck till he was dead. And the street where this happened is named La Calle de la Cabeza, the Street of the Head.

64

The Lovelorn Pig

ONCE there was a young man named Duncan who lived in the little Scottish settlement of Strathalbyn on Prince Edward Island. From childhood on through many years he loved a girl named Flora.

They were sweethearts and playmates, sweethearts in school, and sweethearts when school years were over. The whole village thought they would surely marry.

But before they ever married, Duncan fell in love with another girl. He courted her ardently and soon they were happily married.

Flora took sick soon after this and before the year was out she was dead. She never said a word about Duncan and his new love, but everybody knew that Flora had died of a broken heart.

Not long after this, one day as Duncan was walking along, he felt as if he were being followed. He looked back. He was. It was a pig.

This happened again and again. Duncan would look behind him—and there was the pig, following.

The pig followed Duncan even when he was driving. He would be driving along in his horse and buggy, and there would be the pig, trotting along behind. It never got tired and he could never drive fast enough to leave it behind.

After a while this began to get on Duncan's nerves. He wasn't frightened. He just couldn't stand it! I guess nobody would really *like* being followed by a pig—all the time—everywhere!

One day he was driving along at a good clip—and looked back. Sure enough, there was the pig—running along behind at the same brisk pace.

So he stopped, got out, took the whip from its socket on the dashboard, and gave the pig two or three good licks with it.

The pig ran off into the bushes, and Duncan was startled to hear Flora's sad voice say, "Oh, Duncan, how could you?"

The Ghostly Crew

I'VE tossed about on Georges, been fishing in the Bay,
Out south in early summer—most anywhere would pay.
I've been in different vessels to the Western Bank and Grand,
Likewise in herring vessels that sail to Newfoundland. . . .

One night as we were sailing, we were off land a way—
I never shall forget it until my dying day—
It was in our dim dark watches I felt a chilly dread
Come over me as though I heard one calling from the dead.

68

Right o'er our rail came climbing, all silent, one by one,
A dozen dripping sailors. Just wait till I am done.
Their faces pale and sea-wet shone ghostly through the night.
Each fellow took his station as if he had a right.

They moved about before us till land did heave in sight—
Or rather, I should say so—the light of Tower Light.
And then those ghostly sailors moved to the rail straightway
And vanished like the misty scud before the break of day.

Then we sailed into harbor, and every mother's son
Can tell you this same story, the same as I have done.

The trip before the other, we were on Georges then,
We ran down another vessel and sank her and her men.

Those were the same poor fellows—I hope God rest their souls—
That our old craft ran under that night on Georges Shoals.
Well now my song is ended; it is just as I say,
I do believe in spirits—since that time anyway.

· · ·

The Banks are a great underwater plateau in the Atlantic Ocean which stretch 1,100 miles from Nantucket to the east and south of Newfoundland. These are the most famous codfishing grounds in the world. Georges Bank lies off Cape Cod; the Western Bank lies southeast of Nova Scotia; the Grand Bank lies south and east of Newfoundland.

That drowned sailors always climb aboard the vessel from which they were lost whenever it returns to or crosses the spot where they were lost is a deep-rooted belief among seagoing people. They believe, too—as in this ballad—that they also climb aboard the vessel which ran theirs down when it comes back to that place.

From *Shantymen and Shantyboys: Songs of the Sailor and Lumberman* by William M. Doerflinger, The Macmillan Company, 1951. By permission of the publishers.

The Ghostly Hitchhiker

ONE evening a bus was going along a highway in Illinois between towns, and a young woman stepped out from the side of the road and signaled it.

The driver stopped and the woman got in. But she had no fare. She explained to the driver that it was late and too far to walk. And she just *had* to get home. She was only going to the next town and she mentioned a street and house number. She was hatless and coatless and seemed so worried and upset that the driver let her ride.

The woman sat down in a rear seat and the bus drove on. The woman sitting beside her tried to pick up conversation with her, but the newcomer was not talkative. She answered politely, but with as few words as possible.

The bus slowed up somewhat just before crossing the bridge over the little river which skirted the next town. Passengers began to pick up packages and jackets, getting ready to get off.

Suddenly the passenger in the back seat noticed that her new companion was no longer there. She looked everywhere, up and down the bus, but the young woman was nowhere in sight.

As she got off, she told the driver that the young woman he had picked up on the highway had disappeared.

That was funny, he thought. He had not stopped to let anyone off. There was only the one front door. And the woman just was not there.

That young woman sure was in trouble, he thought, and he decided he had better go to the address she mentioned and tell her family what had happened.

He found the house and rang the bell. A sad-looking woman came to the door and asked what he wanted. He described the worried girl he had picked up on the highway and who had disappeared.

"That was my daughter," said the old woman. "She died right here this evening at seven-thirty."

That was exactly the time the driver had stopped the bus and picked her up.

Aunt Tilly

THE house was a beautiful, big old house on the Eastern Shore of Maryland, standing well back from the water in a setting of gardens and trees. There, almost a hundred years ago, the members of a well-known old family were gathered together for one of its many big family parties.

Every relation for miles around always came to these celebrations, which were held without fail for the birthdays, anniversaries, comings-out, weddings, and christenings of its members.

This time it was summertime, full summer rosetime. Everybody was there. The story does not say whether this was somebody's birthday, or what. But everybody was there, everybody—except Aunt Tilly.

Aunt Tilly lived fifteen miles down the shore. She had already sent word that she was ill that day and could not come.

Late in the afternoon, tea was being served in the big room. One of the ladies was standing in the window looking out at the roses and suddenly said, "Why, there's Tilly now! She came after all!"

Others looked out and saw Aunt Tilly walking slowly through the rose garden. She stopped a moment, as if about to come up the path to the house, looked up at them and smiled, and then turned away and walked slowly into the trees.

They called her name, but she did not look back or answer. They ran out and searched through the gardens, but she was not there. Two hours went by and she was not found.

Then came a messenger from Aunt Tilly's household, bearing word that Aunt Tilly had died that afternoon.

The moment of her death was the moment when she stood and smiled at them from the rose garden. Aunt Tilly had come to the party.

The Cradle That Rocked by Itself

THERE was a raging storm at sea. The wind howled and lashed around many a snug house in many a little town up and down the coast of Maine. Many a ship at sea was in trouble that night, and some were never heard from again.

"I hear a baby crying out there," said a woman in one warm kitchen in one of those little towns. But the rest of the family said it was the wind howling, or seals, maybe, for a frightened baby seal often cries like a baby.

The woman said no, she knew in her heart it was a baby.

"How *could* it be?" said the others.

Nobody went out to look.

The next morning they found a cradle washed ashore, out of some ship. And they took it up to the house, for it was a good cradle. And they used it for every baby that came along, year after year.

But there was one strange thing about it: every time the wind blew a gale the cradle would rock by itself.

All by itself in the warm room, with the wind roaring outside, the cradle would rock just as if someone were sitting by it gently rocking a child.

This happened so often that the family got used to it. No harm ever came of it, and the baby liked it. So they just got used to it and didn't mind.

Then one time the woman's sister came to visit. As they were setting the table for supper one night, the sister glanced into the next room.

"Who is that woman rocking the cradle?" she said.

"Woman? That's no woman. The cradle rocks by itself."

"It is too a woman," said the sister. "She has long black hair and her face is white and sad, and she's sitting there rocking the cradle and bending over the baby."

Nobody else could see her. But the mother grabbed up her baby. And the next day they took the cradle outdoors and chopped it up for kindling wood.

And when the wood was burning in the fire, they could hear some baby crying—somewhere—crying and crying for its cradle.

But after that they never heard it again.

The Gangster in the Back Seat

ONCE a young couple, out shopping for an old used car, wandered into a used-car lot and began to look over what was there. Suddenly they came upon a late-model Packard standing among the old wrecks.

It shone. It gleamed. It looked perfect.

They asked the price, never for a minute expecting to be able to buy it. The price was ridiculously low. The car seemed absolutely perfect. All right. They would buy it.

"You don't want that car," said the manager of the lot.

Oh, but they did!

"Everybody buys it brings it back!" he said.

But they bought it. They could not imagine ever giving it up.

And they were just as delighted after the car was theirs. They took long blissful rides together. They could hardly believe their luck.

But the first time either of them went out alone (usually the young wife) it was another story.

The first time the young woman drove the car by herself, she kept feeling as if someone were in the back seat. She would turn her head and look, and of course no one was there. But the feeling persisted.

One day as she glanced in the rear-view mirror she saw two ugly, leering eyes looking right into hers.

She stopped the car and turned to look. But there was no one there.

Sometimes she would smell the heavy smell of a strong cigar. But when she looked, there was no one there.

The young woman said nothing of all this to her husband. He too would see the face in the mirror or smell the cigar. But they never said a word to each other.

Time went by and the lone driver began to hear the voice of this back-seat ghost: an ugly voice, ugly words—never a full sentence.

The day finally came when neither one could stand it any longer. They confessed their experiences to each other and they took the car back.

"You saw him, too, huh?" said the used-car dealer. "Couldn't stand that cigar, huh?"

"Who *is* he?" the young couple asked.

And the story ends with the terrifying gangster in the back seat being some well-known hood of the Al Capone empire, who had been taken for the proverbial ride and rubbed out in his own car—that very car. And so the car turned up in the used-car lot—again and again and again. Every buyer was terrified of the terrifying face in the rear-view mirror and terrified of the terrifying voice.

Everyone who bought it brought it back.

Oral Americana contributed by Macdonald H. Leach.

Ghost Games

The Devil in the Dishes

TO PLAY this game one child must be the mother. She can have any number of children.

One by one she sends them off on some errand.

The first child starts off, and comes back very frightened.

"I can't go! I can't go! There's something out there *chap, chap, chapping!*"

MOTHER: "Oh, that's nothing! It's daddy's breeches on the line *flap, flap, flapping!*"

And she chooses a second child to go with the first and keep her company. So the two disappear and in a few minutes come running back, terrified.

"We can't go! We can't go! There's something out there *chap, chap, chapping!*"

MOTHER: "Oh, that's nothing, you silly children! That's nothing but the ducks *a-quack, quack, quacking.*"

This time she sends a third child along with the other two so they will not be afraid.

The three go off together then. But in a minute all three run back to the mother, scared to death.

"We can't go! We can't go! There's something out there *chap, chap, chapping!*"

MOTHER: "Well, let's go see what it is!"

So the mother goes to look, followed by all the children. They see no one, but they hear the *chap, chap, chapping.*

Suddenly they find the Devil. The Devil is another child who has been hidden, clapping and scraping two little stones together.

They all yell, "The Devil's in the dishes!" And everybody chases the Devil until he is caught.

Old Roger

HERE is a good singing game. Any number can play. One child has to be chosen to be Old Roger, who is laid in his grave; one has to represent the tree at the head of Old Roger's grave; and one has to come forth to pick the apples that fall from the tree.

Old Roger lies down on the ground (or floor) with a handkerchief over his face. All the others join hands and form a circle around him.

The circle can stand still while the words are sung, or the children can move slowly and solemnly around him.

Here is the tune of the song:

—Earls Heaton (H. Hardy).

Here are the words:

> Old Roger is dead and is laid in his grave
> > Laid in his grave
> > Laid in his grave
> Old Roger is dead and is laid in his grave
> > Hey! Hi!
> > Laid in his grave.

> They planted an apple tree over his head
> > Over his head
> > Over his head
> They planted an apple tree over his head
> > Hey! Hi!
> > Over his head.

While the second verse is being sung, one child steps out of the ring and stands at Old Roger's head to be the tree. She can hold her arms out to be branches if she wishes.

The apples got ripe and they all fell off
They all fell off
They all fell off
The apples got ripe and they all fell off
Hey! Hi!
They all fell off.

There came an old woman a-picking them up
Picking them up
Picking them up
There came an old woman a-picking them up
Hey! Hi!
Picking them up.

While this verse is being sung another child steps out of the
circle and pretends to pick up the apples.

Old Roger jumped up and gave her a knock
Gave her a knock
Gave her a knock
Old Roger jumped up and gave her a knock
Hey! Hi!
Gave her a knock.

The child playing the old woman screams and wails and runs
off limping, while the children in the ring sing:

And made the old woman go hipperty-hop
Hipperty-hop
Hipperty-hop

And made the old woman go hipperty-hop
Hey! Hi!
Hipperty-hop.

As soon as the old woman goes off limping and screaming, Old Roger starts in on the others, chasing and beating them until they all run away screaming and hobbling.

Ghost

ANY number of children can play this game, but one must be the mother; one must be the eldest daughter; one must be the next eldest daughter; and one must be the ghost. All the rest are the mother's other children.

The ghost is chosen and then goes to hide in a corner.

ELDEST DAUGHTER: "Mother, Mother, I want a piece of bread and butter."

MOTHER: "Let's see your hands. My goodness, they are dirty!"

ELDEST DAUGHTER: "I will go wash them."

She goes toward the corner where the ghost is hiding, and the ghost pops up and scares her. She runs back, crying:

"Mother! Mother! I saw a ghost!"

"Nonsense, child! That was just your father's nightshirt flapping on the line."

The mother then tells the next child to go with her so she won't be scared.

They both walk toward the corner, and again the ghost pops up and scares them. They run back.

87

"Mother! Mother! We saw the ghost!"

"Nonsense, children! There is no such thing!"

The mother then picks up a stick or something to represent a candle or a lantern and says, "Let's all go together and find it."

All the players then go toward the corner where the ghost is hiding. The ghost pops up with a terrible screech and chases the whole bunch, who run off screaming here and there. The first one she catches is the ghost for the next game.

Witch Stories

Witch Cat

ONCE there was a young man named Kowashi, who lived with his old mother in a small Japanese village at the foot of a mountain. They were happy, respectable people and lived their lives in the simple good way.

There was just one thing the young man used to wonder about. His mother used to be a gentle, sweet little woman. But when she got to be about eighty years old, he began to notice that she had long, sharp pointed teeth. She used to eat her fish raw and even seemed to enjoy crunching up the raw bones.

One night a fish peddler of that village was walking home through the mountain pass after a day's work at the market. He had not sold all his fish that day. And those left over were in the fish basket which he carried on a pole over his shoulder.

He was not afraid of night robbers, because it was a bright moonlight night and he could see every stick and stone in the path.

Suddenly he was set upon by a whole horde of cats. They smelled the fish in his basket and were determined to get it.

He fought them off with the long pole. And he fought so

smartly that finally the cats gave up the fight. Then one of
them said: "Go call Old Woman Kowashi."

"That's funny," the peddler said to himself, for young Kowashi
and his mother were his neighbors in the village.

So the man quickly climbed into a pine tree, wondering what
would happen next.

It was a bright moonlight night and the man could see the
path and all the cats and their shadows as plain as day.

Soon one of the cats said, "Here she comes."

Another said, "Here comes Old Woman Kowashi."

The man looked. And what he saw was a big, tough, old gray
cat coming through the pass.

92

"He won't give us the fish!" all the cats said together.

So the big gray cat climbed up into the fish peddler's tree. He was lying stretched out along a branch. The cat crawled out along the same branch until she came to him—eye to eye!

Inch by inch she came nearer. Each of her sharp claws looked six inches long.

What could he do?

Suddenly he remembered that he had his fish gaff with him. (A fish gaff is a heavy barbed hook with a wooden handle used for hauling heavy fish into a boat after they are hooked.)

Quickly he grabbed the fish gaff and gave the big gray cat a whack on the head.

Just about then the sun peeked over the horizon. It was morning and all the cats instantly vanished. One minute they were there, and the next minute they were gone—just like that.

The fish peddler climbed down from the tree and hurried home. And that morning he went and told young Kowashi the whole story.

The young man listened and nodded his head. He had noticed a cut on his mother's head that morning! He had asked her what caused it, and she explained that she had stumbled and hit her head on a stone in the garden.

But young Kowashi suddenly understood. So he took his long sword and cut off her head at one stroke.

Then he looked down and what lay at his feet was a bloody old gray cat.

Not long after this Kowashi discovered that the wicked old witch had killed his real mother and buried her in the garden.

Sop, Doll!

ONCE there was a miller who owned a big mill. And he hired a young boy named Jack to help him.

The day Jack arrived, he said, "I've come to tend the mill."

And the miller said, "Well, I must tell you that I've had many millers and they all died the first night."

"All right," said Jack. "I don't care."

"Just the man I need!" said the miller.

So he showed Jack all around the mill. And he showed him his own corner where he would sleep and the fireplace where he would cook. And he showed him his own store of meal and meat and his own big skillet.

This was fine, Jack thought, and he set right to to bake some bread and fry some meat. And then he sat down on the floor to eat his meat and bread and gravy, or sop, as gravy was called in that region. A candle on the table and the blazing fire made light enough.

Then all of a sudden it got pitch-dark.

Jack leaned forward to stir up his fire for more light, and when he sat back the mill was full of cats. He couldn't count all the yellow eyes a-shining in the dark.

He felt sort of scared, but he began to eat his supper.

Then one old cat stepped out in front of Jack and said, "Sop, doll, sop!"

All the cats sat down in rows in front of Jack then. And the big old cat stuck her paw in Jack's meat sop and licked it.

"Sop, doll, sop!" she yelled.

Jack did feel pretty scared, but he said, "You stick your paw in here again and I'll whack it off!"

So she stuck her paw in Jack's meat sop again and licked it.

"Sop, doll, sop!" she yelled.

"Do that again and I'll whack it off!" said Jack.

So she did it again and so Jack whacked it off.

The old cat gave a great screech and disappeared, and all the cats vanished with her.

The paw had fallen right into the skillet, and Jack saw that it was not a paw but a woman's hand with a fine gold ring on it. So Jack took the hand and wiped the meat sop off it and put it in his pocket and went to sleep.

In the morning he went to the house to tell the miller what had happened. The miller was glad to see that Jack was still alive.

"Oh, sure, I'm alive," said Jack.

So Jack told the miller his story and pulled the hand with the ring on it out of his pocket. And the miller saw that it was his own wife's hand and his own wife's ring which he had given her himself.

He ran upstairs to find her and found her lying in bed very sick.

96

"Show me your ring," he said.

And the woman stretched her left hand out of the covers with an old dull ring on it.

"The other one!" said the miller.

But she wouldn't.

So he grabbed up her right arm himself and saw that the hand had been cut off at the wrist.

Then the miller knew that his wife was a witch.

Singing Bone

ONCE there was a cruel witch who sent her little girl up the hill to pick pears.

"And don't give any away!" she said.

Then she dressed herself up in old rags and hurried to the place and picked all the pears herself before the little girl could get there.

When the little girl got there, there was just one pear left hanging on one tree. So she picked that and started home.

On the way she met a miserable old woman who begged her for the pear. The old woman was really the cruel mother in disguise trying to make the little girl disobey.

"Oh, please gimme just one little pear," she begged.

"I can't! I can't!" said the little girl. "My mother said not to." But the old woman kept begging and begging, and finally the little girl felt so sorry for her that she gave her the pear.

When she got home, of course, she had no pears.

"So you gave them all away!" said the woman.

"Some one stole them before I got there," said the little girl. "There was only one."

"Come lay your head in my lap, dear," said the woman.

The little girl did and the cruel woman cut off her head with the kitchen knife. Then she took the head outdoors and buried it in the potato patch. She made stew for supper out of the rest.

But she did not get all the little girl's hair covered up. Some curls were left sticking up out of the ground.

When she sent the little boy down to the potato patch to dig some potatoes for supper, he saw the hair and started to pull it.

Brother, brother, don't pull my hair!
Mother killed me for a single pear!

The little boy heard the song and could not believe his ears. So he pulled the hair again. Again he heard his sister's voice sing:

Brother, brother, don't pull my hair!
Mother killed me for a single pear!

So he ran into the house and said he couldn't dig those potatoes. "Oh, well, *you* go," said the woman to the father.

So the father went out to the potato patch to get potatoes and saw the hair.

Father, father, don't pull my hair!
Mother killed me for a single pear!

So he turned around and ran into the house and killed the wicked woman.

Do's and Don't's
About Ghosts

Signs of Ghosts

SOME people get scary feelings and begin to wonder if there are ghosts about. But you don't have to wonder. There are ways of telling! All through the centuries our ancestors have taken certain little signs and happenings as tokens that a ghost is present.

When the little flame of a candle burns blue, it is a sign that a ghost is present.

If a bat flies into the house, it is a sign that ghosts are about. In fact, it has probably come in *with* one.

Cats crossing your path are a sign of ghosts. Some say it has to be a black cat, and some say any old cat. But a black cat is often either a witch or a ghost and can put a spell on you.

If you are walking along a road at night and hear a stick break, that was a ghost.

A little tiny whirlwind of dust on the ground is the sign of a ghost's passing.

If you are walking along a road at night and come into a current of hot air, you have walked into a ghost.

Ghosts are luminous. They give off a glowing kind of light. If you stare at it, it will vanish.

If you see lights moving about and they disappear when you approach them, they were ghosts.

Lights moving around in a graveyard are ghosts for sure.

The jack-o'-lantern or will-o'-the-wisp is a ghost, they say. It is the soul of someone dead who has returned to earth in the shape of a ball of fire. Don't follow it. It loves to lead people into swamps. In case you do get tricked into following it, quick turn your jacket (or shirt) inside out and the spell will be broken. Or if you stick your knife into the ground and hold onto it, you'll be safe.

If you are talking to someone in the wintertime and suddenly notice that he (or she) has living green birch leaves in his hat, you are talking to a ghost. When the dead return to earth for

106

some reason, they often wear birch leaves as a kind of token that they will return to the other world.

Ghosts cast no shadow. That's one sure sign. So if you have been talking to someone some bright moonlight night and notice that he has no shadow—you have been talking to a ghost!

Charms Against Ghosts

IF YOU have to go walking alone along some road at night, *always* carry a piece of bread crust in your pocket or somewhere about you. This will not only protect you from ghosts and other frightening things. It will even keep you from being afraid.

If you see a ghost and are brave enough to walk around it nine times, it will go away.

If you have to pass by a haunted place at night, turn your pockets inside out and the ghost won't hurt you.

In England and in the United States they say that a ghost will never approach a light left burning in a room at night. And candlelight especially is a powerful protection.

Cockcrow, that is, daybreak, is a charm against ghosts, because all ghosts, witches, zombies, and other frightening night-roaming beings have to disappear the minute the cock crows, the minute the first ray of daylight touches the earth.

If you are troubled with ghosts in the home, strew ashes on the floor. The next day you can see their footprints in the ashes, and they won't come back.

Ringing bells and beating on pots and pans will usually make ghosts depart in a hurry. They can't stand the noise. Church bells especially will make ghosts go away.

Ghosts can be gotten rid of by bidding them begone by name.

If ever a ghost gets after you, jump across a brook or jump into a small boat and row out to midstream, or run across a bridge, for it is well-known that ghosts can't cross running water.

If you are walking in a country lane some night and see a ghost, the thing to do is *cross the lane*. No ghost or evil spirit can cross a lane. All old country people know that. Once in a lane a ghost is in a fix: it has to keep going. So just jump out of the lane!

Always carry a key, because you can always get rid of a ghost by throwing a key at it. This is an old English belief and common in the United States.

Carrying a knife also protects you against ghosts. They are afraid of being cut.

If you carry with you a piece of holly picked on Christmas, ghosts cannot harm you. Holly is evergreen and ghosts have no power against it.

A wire screen or a mosquito net will keep ghosts out. In fact, screens, nets, and sieves are age-old ghost barriers in both the Old and New World. Hang a sieve over a keyhole and no ghost or witch can get in. The explanation is that they have to stop and count every hole in a screen (or a net or a sieve), and thus daybreak comes before they have finished counting and they have to depart. But whether they really *do* this or not—who knows?

How To See Ghosts or Surely Bring Them To You

THIS part of the book is for children who were born in the morning or around lunch time. If you were born at midnight (some say just at twilight), you were probably born with the gift of being able to see ghosts and other spirits, and don't have to be told how.

Of course, all cats, dogs, horses, and roosters can see ghosts. But lots of people cannot see ghosts (even though they can usually hear them). And lots of people don't believe in ghosts because they say they never saw one!

So—anyone who wants to see a ghost—here's how!

If you really mean it—if you really *want to see* a ghost—go walk around a grave twelve times backward, and the ghost will rise and ask you what you want. Some people say that just walking around the grave will raise the ghost, and some say you have to do it backward twelve times. Or—if you want to summon some one particular ghost—go to his grave at night and *call him by name.* He will rise and tell you what you want to know.

Some ghosts can be summoned by music. If you sing or play some piece of music or some special musical instrument that someone loved especially during life, the ghost will come to you.

Some people say that you can raise a ghost by whistling. You might and you might not. It *has* happened. Once a man was walking along a road at night, whistling some tune, and a ghost fell into step beside him, whistling the same tune.

You can call back some loved ghost by too much grief and weeping. Almost any ghost will come back to comfort those they love and stop their weeping. The poor souls cannot rest if you weep too much. They will come back and beg you to let them rest.

You can become a ghost-seer by looking in through a hole in a coffin. This is especially true in some far northern countries, like Lithuania, for instance, where people leave little windows in the coffins so the dead can see out.

You can see ghosts and spirits by peering at them from between a dog's ears. It is well-known that dogs can see ghosts. So if you

look steadily from between a dog's ears, in the direction the dog is looking, you will see the same ghost he sees.

You can see ghosts sometimes if you gaze steadily through a ring. If you look through a keyhole, you'll either see a ghost or the Devil. In fact, there's no telling what you might see. Better not!

Just say you aren't scared! Just say how brave and nonchalant you'd be if you ever saw a ghost—and SEE WHAT HAPPENS.

Don't—

DON'T ever brag about what you'd do if you saw a ghost, or one will surely come!

Don't slam the door, because you might pinch some poor soul in it.

Don't leave sharp knives lying around either, or some wandering spirit or ghost might get cut with them.

Don't go looking over the graveyard wall. If you do, you will see ghosts.

Don't laugh at ghosts. They are no joke.

In Germany they say don't bring an elder branch into the house because ghosts will come in with it.

If ever you come upon an old hat or a piece of clothing lying

on the ground with a stick across it, don't pick it up. The stick
is a sign that it belongs to a ghost. Don't touch it.

Don't yawn without covering your mouth with your hand.
Ghosts are attracted by yawning. Some people say they will peer
in and count your teeth (or your fillings!). But a very common
belief in the world is that your soul can slip out when you yawn,
and some ghost can slip in. If this happens, you will sicken and
die.

Don't ever speak to a ghost unless you really want it to answer,
because ghosts *have to answer* as soon as spoken to.

Don't Ever Kick a Ghost

ONCE there was a man going along a road one night, on his way home from somewheres. He was going along, going along. He had to walk past the fields, past the houses, past the church, past the graveyard, before he came to his own place.

And just as he was passing by the graveyard he saw something white lying in the road ahead. It was about the size of a possum, he said. When he came up to it he gave it a kick, and it was suddenly as big as a dog.

"That's funny!" the man said to himself, and kicked it again. The white thing swelled up as big as a cow.

That man was so scared, he ran and ran and ran. He must have got home at last because the word passed round the town

DON'T EVER KICK A GHOST!

Author's Notes and Bibliography

The abbreviations used in this section are: *CAF (California Folklore Quarterly)*, *JAF (Journal of American Folklore)*, *MAFS (Memoirs of the American Folklore Society)*, *NMFR (New Mexico Folklore Record)*. The numbers in parentheses are the motif numbers as given in Stith Thompson's *Motif Index of Folk Literature*.

FUNNY ONES

The Thing at the Foot of the Bed. My grandfather used to tell this story as having actually happened somewhere in Shelburne County, Nova Scotia, when he was a young boy. The tale is also current in rural America. Toes mistaken for ghost and shot off is motif J1782.8; things thought at night to be other frightful object is motif J1789.

Here We Go! This is a famous story in the north of England, especially in Lancashire, but according to Harland and Wilkinson, it is also familiar in most of northern Europe. It contains a number of motifs common in the British Isles, Canada, and the United States: spirits pull off bedclothes (F470.1); spirit puts out lights (F473.2.3); ghost (spirit) makes rapping noise (E402.1.5); helpful deeds of household spirit (F482.5.4); brownie (boggart) sticks head out of churn on top of wagon and says, "Yes, we're flitting!" (F482.3.1.1).

Ghost Race. The story of the racing ghost is a Negro tale known and told almost everywhere (with minor variations) throughout the West Indies and in the southern United States. It is especially popular in the South from Alabama eastward and northward to South Carolina, Virginia, Philadelphia, and New York. And two variants of the tale were told to Arthur H. Fauset by Negroes in Nova Scotia.

One of the funniest and most famous of the ghost-race tales is the Alabama version collected by Dr. Fauset and published in his "Negro Folk Tales from the South," *JAF* 40:259. "Never Mind Them Watermelons" is based on this version. "The Guitar Player" is based on a Surinam Negro story collected in the city of Paramaribo (Dutch Guiana) by Melville J. and Frances S. Herskovits: *Suriname Folk-Lore*, pp. 427-428. The motifs in this tale are ghost travels swiftly (E599.5) and ghost converses with man running from him (J1495.1).

Wait Till Martin Comes. This is a very old, very well-known Negro folktale reported in various versions from Mississippi, West Virginia, Alabama, and South Carolina. This telling is based on two versions collected by John Harrington Cox in West Virginia and published in his article "Negro Folktales from West Virginia," *JAF* 47:352-353 (1934). In one of these the cats are waiting for Emmett, in the other for Martin. In the telling reported by Arthur H. Fauset from Alabama (*JAF* 40:258-259) they are waiting for Patience. In a tale from South Carolina reported by Howard W. Odum they are waiting for Whalem-Balem. Still another current name turns up in motif J1495.2: wait till Caleb comes, reported by E. W. Baughman in his "Comparative Study of the Folktales of England and North America," Indiana University dissertation, 1954.

Big Fraid and Little Fraid. This story is widely told all over the southern United States, with varying details, by Negroes and whites alike. Versions have been published from Missouri, Louisiana, the Kentucky mountains, Florida, North Carolina, Virginia, New Jersey, and Ontario. Arthur H. Fauset found it being told also among Southern Negroes in Philadelphia. It embodies motif K1682.1: disguised trickster is himself frightened. The telling presented here follows no one particular variant but represents the detail and spirit of all.

The Lucky Man. This story is based on the age-old numskull tale about the Turkish noodle named Khoja Nasreddin who is said to have lived about the middle of the fourteenth century.

In the story as told in Clouston's *Book of Noodles,* p. 90, he mistook his own caftan (a long-sleeved gown worn by men of the region) for a thief, shot it full of holes, and upon discovering his mistake made the famous remark that it was lucky he wasn't in it or he would have shot himself. Fool would have shot himself is motif J2235.

The anecdote is often told of the proverbial Irishman and his famous linguistic nonsense. It was popular, too, in the 1930s as one of the Little Moron stories.

SCARY ONES

The Golden Arm. Arthur H. Fauset reports a related Negro formula tale from Truro, Nova Scotia, in which a tiny old woman finds a tiny bone in a tiny church, takes it home, and puts it under her tiny pillow. When a tiny voice wails for the bone in the night, she gets up and gives it back. No mention is made of this one being a windy-night story.

Leonard Roberts reports the golden-arm story from the West Virginia mountains about two brothers, one of whom had a golden arm. In a North Carolina variant the story is told of two sisters, one of whom takes the diamond ring from her dead sister's hand, after promising not to. The dead one returns for it, and this story, too, ends with the pounce line: You've got it!

The story is classified as a ghost story based on motif E235.4.1: return from the dead to punish theft of golden arm. The diamond-ring version bears motif E236.1.1.

The Dare. This story is so well-known and so widespread that I have followed no specific version or variant in the telling presented here.

The *Frank C. Brown Collection of North Carolina Folklore* (vol. 1, p. 686) reports the tale from Randolph County, North Carolina, in which an old woman scoffs at the warning and takes the dare to go stick a fork in a certain grave at midnight. She does it—but sticks the fork through her own skirt and dies of fright when she cannot get away. Dr. Ralph S. Boggs reports two variants, also from North Carolina, which are printed in his collection "North Carolina White Folktales and Riddles," *JAF* 47:269-328 (1934).

Marcia Klein of Albuquerque, New Mexico, reported the story as having come from Hungary. It was told to her by her Hungarian grandfather as a boyhood escapade of his own, in which he himself lost courage and ran home. But his young chum went through with the dare, pounded a stake through his own coattail, pinned himself to the grave, and died of fright. Miss Klein's telling is printed in *NMFR* 6:27 (1951-1952). A variant, also from Albuquerque, reports a small boy going into a church at midnight to drive a nail into the church floor —with the traditional result (*NMFR* 7:23, 1952-1953).

Majel Fritz of East Moline, Illinois, heard this tale during a storytelling session in Nevada, in which the daredevil goes to the cemetery to thrust a sword into a certain grave in order to win two rubies. In the dark he thrust the sword through his own coattail and died of fright when he could not get away. This was published in *NMFR* 7:23-24 (1952-1953).

Dr. Vance Randolph presents a Missouri variant in a story called "The Infidel's Grave," in *Midwest Folklore* 2:83 (1952). In this variant it was a young girl who took the dare, went to the grave at midnight to drive a croquet stake into it, did not see in the dark that she was driving it through her own skirt, and died of fright when she felt herself "grabbed."

The story is reported to be as well-known and as widely told in England and Ireland as in the United States. The motif is N384.2 (death in the graveyard:

person's clothing caught; he thinks something awful is holding him and dies of fright).

I'm in the Room! This story is retold from the experience of Mrs. Rosie Altrano, reported in *Gumbo Ya-Ya,* p. 277.

No Head. This story is based on and expanded from a Georgia Negro folktale collected by Arthur H. Fauset in Philadelphia and published as #28 in his "Tales and Riddles Collected in Philadelphia," *JAF* 41:544 (1928). Headless revenant (E422.1.1) and return from the dead to reveal hidden treasure (E371) are the specific motifs. That the dead cannot speak until spoken to is motif E545.19.2.

As Long As This? This is a Negro story from Dutch Guiana collected by Melville J. and Frances S. Herskovits in the city of Paramaribo in 1928-1929, and published in their *Suriname Folk-Lore,* p. 427. Jamaica Negroes tell almost the same story about a man in a dark street who asked another for a light, not knowing it was a *duppy* (ghost) he was asking. The duppy's teeth were like fire. He "gashed" them at the man and the man ran. This tale is in Martha Warren Beckwith's "Jamaica Anansi Stories," *MAFS* 17:180 (1924). The duppy with fiery teeth belongs in the general category of ghosts with fiery eyes, fiery tongues, etc., although it is often ghostly dogs or horses which are seen with fiery tongues or eyes.

The Legs. This is a well-known story based on motif E373.1: money from ghost received as reward for bravery. It is well-known in northern Europe—Sweden, Estonia, Lithuania, and Finland—also in Arabia and in India (Madras). And as motif H1411 (fear test: staying in haunted house where corpse drops piece-meal down chimney) it is known in Germany and Denmark; it also turns up in Sir Walter Scott's *Marmion* and in a long elaborate tale entitled "Without Fear" collected by Elsie Clews Parsons in the Cape Verde Islands.

Talk. This story is based on a Florida Negro folktale entitled "High Walker and Bloody Bones" in Zora Neale Hurston's *Mules and Men,* p. 219. High Walker is a Negro slave in this story, however, who tells the tale to his white master and gets his own head cut off for his insistence. It is also based on the version which Arthur H. Fauset found current among Philadelphia Negroes from Alabama. By 1923, however, they were telling it about an old man who happened upon the skull in the road, as here. Dr. Fauset presented his version in "Tales and Riddles Collected in Philadelphia," *JAF* 41:536-537 (1928). It contains the famous speaking-skull motif E261.1.2.

Dark, Dark, Dark. This story was also picked up by Dr. Arthur H. Fauset from a Negro schoolboy in New Glasgow, Nova Scotia. He presented it as a nursery tale in his "Folklore from Nova Scotia," *MAFS* 24:39 (1931).

REAL ONES

Sweet William's Ghost is ballad #77 in the great collection of *English and Scottish Popular Ballads* of Francis J. Child. It is presented here with no changes except a few simplifications of the dialect.

The ballad embodies several beliefs about ghosts which still persist in the human mind, now traditional motifs of folk narrative. One is return from the dead to ask back love tokens or troth (E311). The belief is that the dead cannot rest until relieved of promises they cannot fulfill. Others are: revenant with cold lips (E422.1.4); a kiss from the dead would be fatal (E217); and ghost laid at cockcrow (E452); and taboo: supernatural creature being abroad after sunrise (C752.2.1).

Milk Bottles. This story was told to Pauline H. Barton in 1927, she reports, by her old Negro nurse, Mary Ann Hatcher, who heard it from *her* grandmother, years before that, in Alabama. It was published in *NMFR* 5:34-35 (1902).

The story of the dead mother's friendly return (E323) is very widely known, especially in Europe: in Germany, France, Scandinavia, Lithuania, for instance. The spread of this motif covers not only northern Europe but extends also to India, China, Africa, and turns up too in New World Negro lore. In many tales using the motif of the ghost who returns to aid the living (E363) the mother returns to suckle her child (E323.1). Although the baby in this Alabama Negro story was fed out of a milk bottle, the identity of the old motif in a new dress is obvious. Ghost travels swiftly (E599.5) is also involved.

The Head. This story, of course, is one of the many, many folktales in the world in which murder is always and inevitably punished: murder will out (N271). It is based on and expanded from a tale entitled *La Cabeza* (The Head) in the collection of Puerto Rican folktales published by J. Alden Mason and Aurelio M. Espinosa in *JAF* 40:414 (1927). There are Mexican and New Mexican versions of this Spanish tale in which the murderer buys a pumpkin which so terrifyingly turns into the blood-dripping head of his old friend. The specific motif is Q551.3.3.

The Lovelorn Pig. This story was told as a true story to Helen Creighton by Neil Matheson, M.P., and reported in her *Bluenose Ghosts,* p. 206.

The motifs involved, still current in human belief, are: dead sweetheart haunts faithless lover (E211), revenant in animal form (E423), and ghost travels swiftly (E599.5).

This telling of the tale is based on and somewhat expanded from Miss Creighton's report.

The Ghostly Crew is known and sung from Cape Ann to Cape Race. The version here given is a composite of the two versions given by William M. Doerflinger in *Shantymen and Shantyboys: Songs of the Sailor and Lumberman,* pp. 180-183. It was written by Harry L. Marcy and first published in *Fishermen's Ballads and Songs of the Sea,* Proctor Brothers, Gloucester, Mass., 1874.

The Ghostly Hitchhiker. This is a rather unusual variant of the ghostly hitchhiker story, which is said to be the most popular and widespread ghost story in the United States. It is an old European tale said to have turned up in America about 1890. Dr. Louis C. Jones reported (in 1944) forty-nine versions of it in New York State alone. R. K. Beardsley and R. Hankie in their articles "The Vanishing Hitchhiker," *CFQ* 1:303-336 (1942) and "The History of the Vanishing Hitchhiker," *CFQ* 2:3-25 (1943) reported seventy-nine versions already in print at that time. Versions from Nova Scotia, Jamaica, and Mexico have since been added to the list.

The unique features of the specific tale here given are the motifs: ghost rides bus (E581.4) and disappears before it crosses a bridge (E581.4.1), embodying the almost universal belief that ghosts cannot cross running water (E434.3).

The most usual ghostly hitchhiker tale is told by some motorist who has stopped late at night to pick up a "pretty girl in the road," who asks to be taken home. He drives to the address, discovers that the girl has suddenly vanished, but knocks on the door to inform her family. He is invariably told that the girl died two, four, six years ago, usually in an accident at the spot where he picked her up. Sometimes he goes to the cemetery to verify this information, finds the girl's grave, and on it his own coat (which he has lent her) or the party dress she was wearing.

Aunt Tilly. This story is retold and expanded from a Baltimore newspaper clipping of 1886, reprinted in the Modern Library anthology, *Best Ghost Stories,* pp. 202-203.

The Cradle That Rocked by Itself. This telling of the story of the cradle salvaged from a shipwreck that rocked by itself in every storm is based on the tale, but minus the proper names and the dialect, as presented by Harriet Beecher Stowe in 1862 in *The Pearl of Orr's Island* and reprinted in B. A. Botkin's *Treasury of New England Folklore,* pp. 608-609.

The chair rocked by an invisible spirit (F473.2.1) is found in many a haunted house in the British Isles and has been reported in Nova Scotia (by Helen Creighton, *Bluenose Ghosts*, p. 164); and in the United States from North Carolina in the *Frank C. Brown Collection of North Carolina Folklore* (vol. 1, p. 640); and by Carl Carmer in "The Quaker Girl and the Rocking Ghost," *New York Folklore Quarterly* 11:275 (1955)—a schoolgirl story from Philadelphia told by an old lady in Rochester, New York.

Stories of the cradle rocked by an invisible spirit are less common. The one given here and one reported by Helen Creighton from Victoria Beach, Nova Scotia, are the only ones I have come across.

The Gangster in the Back Seat. This story is, of course, merely the story of the haunted house on wheels, and it is built around the belief that a murdered person cannot rest and haunts the scene of his murder (E413). The story is oral Americana, contributed by Macdonald H. Leach, who says that it is known to people in the automobile business all over the United States, but is believed to have originated in the 1920s in the Cicero-Chicago area during prohibition. Sometimes the car is a Cadillac or a Lincoln; in the earliest stories it was sometimes a Marmon or a Pierce Arrow. Sometimes the tale is told of two college boys or two high-school boys out looking for a jalopy, who buy the magnificent haunted car.

GHOST GAMES

The Devil in the Dishes. This is an old Scottish children's game from Aberdeen, reported by Lady Alice B. Gomme in *Traditional Games of England, Scotland, and Ireland* (vol. 2, p. 413). It is a dramatic game to be acted out—not sung. The original of the line about daddy's breeches gives *drap, drap, drapping.*

Old Roger. This is an old game, classified as a funeral game, formerly much played by English country children. It reflects three things: (1) the ancient European custom of planting a tree at the head of a grave, (2) the belief that the spirit of the dead inhabits the tree, and (3) the belief that the dead rise from the grave to prevent the living from harming the tree or picking its flowers or fruits.

Lady Alice B. Gomme reports twelve variants of the Old Roger game in her *Traditional Games from England, Scotland, and Ireland* (vol. 2, pp. 16-24): eleven from the English shires and one from Belfast, Ireland. She also presents three variants of the tune, of which the one shown here is from Earls Heaton.

Lady Gomme suggests that the game may represent a survival of some old mumming play.

Ghost. This game is reported by Lady Alice B. Gomme in her *Traditional Games of England, Scotland, and Ireland* (vol. 1, p. 149) as an old game played by children in West Cornwall. In London, she says, the children used to shove chairs together to form a tub. The ghost hid in the tub and popped out to scare the one who came to wash clothes in it.

WITCH STORIES

Witch Cat. This story contains a minor variation of the very widespread witch stories in which the witch takes the form of an animal (G211), specifically, the form of a cat (G211.1.7). In most tales, the cat gets its paw cut off, the next morning a certain woman is discovered to have lost a hand and is thus identified as the witch (G252). Motif G214, the witch with extraordinary teeth, and motif C752.2.1, taboo against a supernatural creature being abroad after sunrise are also involved.

The cat's-paw motif is well-known and frequent in the British Isles and Canada, and in almost all the United States. It is also current in western Europe from Lithuania to Spain, and seems to be equally common in Japan. The story from Japan told here, of course, involves all the same motifs, the cut-off paw or the knock on the head being mere variations. As presented here the tale is based on "The Bald-Headed Cat of Kowashi," in Yoshimatsu Suzuki's *Japanese Legends and Folk-Tales,* pp. 18-20.

Sop, Doll! In most versions of the tale about the witch cat in the mill, the woman instantly turns into a cat again, upon discovery, and disappears with a yowl. In some versions the miller kills her or burns down the house with her in it. In the version upon which this telling is based (I. G. Carter's "Mountain White Folk-lore: Tales from the Southern Blue Ridge," *JAF* 38:354) the tale is prolonged by having the miller promise his wife not to burn her for a witch if she will tell the whole truth. All the neighboring witch-cat women are burned, however. The words *sop, doll* mean "gravy, paw." *Sop* means gravy, and *doll* is an old Northumberland dialect word for a little child's hand.

The witch in the form of a cat (G211.1.7) turns up all over Europe and the British Isles and is well-known in American folktale, especially in the South, among both Negroes and whites. Grimm's tales #4 and #69 both contain it. Other more specific motifs in this story are: witch in form of cat has paw cut off; recognition by missing hand (G252.1.1), and witch in animal form is killed or injured as result of injury while in animal form (G275.12). This motif and its twin: cat's paw cut off; woman's hand missing (D702.1.1) are known in the British Isles, Nova Scotia, the United States, India, and Japan.

Sometimes it is a traveler seeking lodging for the night who has the experience in the mill. And the injured part is not always a paw but can be tongue (India), head (Japan), shoulder, back, etc. (U.S.).

The *Frank C. Brown Collection of North Carolina Folklore* (vol. 1, pp. 660-664) presents a long literary version of the tale in which the miller keeps watch in his own mill in order to catch whatever mischief-maker is tearing holes in the meal sacks and spilling the grain, putting nails in the hopper, etc. He is suddenly encircled by a horde of black cats which close in, nearer and nearer. He cuts off the right paw of one of them with an ax, whereupon they all scream and vanish. The miller runs home to tell his wife and finds her in bed with her right hand cut off. She instantly turns into a black cat and disappears.

Richard Chase also collected the Sop, Doll! story in North Carolina and retold it to some length in his *Jack Tales*, pp. 76-82.

Singing Bone. This telling of the singing-bone story is a composite of the Kentucky mountain version given by Leonard Roberts in *South from Hell-fer-Sartin,* pp. 96-97 and the version collected by Arthur H. Fauset from Southern Negroes in Philadelphia (*JAF* 41:537). Elsie Clews Parsons picked up the same tale in New York from a Negro storyteller from Georgia. (See her "Folk-Lore from Georgia," *JAF* 47:388.) In this Georgia variant the woman buried the little girl in the lily bed, and it was the child's dog pulling at the lilies which evoked the song

> *Do, doggie, don't pull my hair!*
> *My mother killed me for a fig and a grape.*

The fruit sought in the southern United States tales and for which the child was killed varies in the many versions: pears, blackberries, figs, grapes, peppers. And sometimes the story begins with the explanation that the cruel woman is a stepmother and a witch.

The motif of the singing bone, i.e. speaking (singing) bones of the victim reveal murder (E632.1) is well-known in the British Isles, all over western Europe, in the Bahamas (here of French and Spanish provenience), and in the southern United States, particularly Louisiana, Missouri, Georgia, South Carolina, and the Kentucky mountains. Grimm's tale *The Juniper Tree* is the well-known European form of the story. Stories of a musical instrument made from the bone of a murdered person (or a singing tree from his grave) which reveals the murder (E632) have the same spread and are also told in India and Japan. The reincarnation of the murdered child as a bird whose song reveals the murder is equally common and is known in all the above-mentioned areas, plus Africa. Other motifs involved are murder will out (N271), murder punished (Q211), cruel stepmother or mother (S12), and quest assigned to get rid of heroine (H1211).

DO'S AND DON'T'S ABOUT GHOSTS

Signs of Ghosts. This section contains the merest handful of human beliefs from various parts of the world about ghosts and how people tell when they are present or about. But they turn up so frequently in folktale and folksong that they have been classified as motifs. They are: light(s) as soul(s) of the dead (A1412.2); ghosts cast no shadow (E421.2); ghosts are luminous (E421.3); cats crossing one's path are signs of ghosts (E436.2); bats flying into the house are signs of ghosts (E436.3); whirlwind of dust: sign of ghost's passing (E581.1); jack-o'-lantern as soul of dead (E742.2).

Charms Against Ghosts. The number of charms and amulets in the world, everywhere in the world, which protect human beings and animals, houses and households, barns and pastures against ghosts, witches, the Devil, and all evil spirits can never be counted. All of them will probably never even be discovered. But a few of the best-known old reliables from northern Europe, the British Isles, and the United States are given here. The assignment of motif numbers to the very few included in this section bears witness to the spread and the strength of human faith in their efficacy. They are: ghosts cannot cross running water (E434.3); keys protect against ghosts (E434.6); knives protect against ghosts (E434.7); candlelight protects against ghosts (E434.7); ghost will vanish if walked around nine times (E439.8); ghost exorcised by name (E443.3); ghost laid at cockcrow (E452); jack-o'-lantern leads astray (F491.1); turn garment inside out as protection against jack-o'-lantern (F491.3.2); sticking knife in ground protects against jack-o'-lantern (F491.1).

How To See Ghosts. The motifs involved in this section are: magic sight by looking between dog's ears (D1821.3.4); . . . by looking through a ring (D1821.3.4); one becomes a ghost-seer by looking through hole in coffin

(D1821.3.5.1.); magic sight by looking through a keyhole (D1821.3.6); ghost summoned by weeping (E381); ghost summoned by music (D384); ghost summoned by whistling (E384.2); ghost summoned by calling by name E386.3); walking around grave (twelve times backward) raises ghost (E386.4); persons born at midnight can see ghosts (E421.1.1); whistling after sunset causes Devil (or ghost) to go along with one (G303.16.18).

Don't—Taboo against certain actions, lest one see ghosts, are so universally rooted in human practice, so frequent and widespread in folktale as well as daily life, that they are identified as motifs. Only a few, out of hundreds, have been picked up here. They are: taboo: looking over cemetery wall lest you see ghosts (C334); taboo: to laugh at a ghost (C462); don't brag about what you would do if you saw a ghost (E386.5); ghost must answer when spoken to (E404.1).

Don't Ever Kick a Ghost. This story is based on a North Carolina village story reported in the *Frank C. Brown Collection of North Carolina Folklore* (vol. 1, p. 675).

BIBLIOGRAPHY

Pauline H. Barton: The Woman in Gray, *New Mexico Folklore Record* 5.34–35 (1950)

Martha Warren Beckwith: Jamaica Anansi Stories, *Memoirs of American Folklore Society* 17:180 (1924)

Best Ghost Stories, Boni & Liveright, Inc., New York, 1919

Ralph S. Boggs: North Carolina Folktales and Riddles, *Journal of American Folklore* 47:269–328 (1934)

Frank C. Brown Collection of North Carolina Folklore, vol. 1, Duke University Press, Durham, 1952

W. A. Clouston: *Book of Noodles,* Elliott Stock, London, 1888

Helen Creighton: *Bluenose Ghosts,* Ryerson Press, Toronto, 1957

William M. Doerflinger: *Shantymen and Shantyboys: Songs of the Sailor and Lumberman,* The Macmillan Company, New York, 1951

Alice Morse Earle: *Child Life in Colonial Days,* The Macmillan Company, New York, 1899

Arthur Huff Fauset: Folklore from Nova Scotia, *Memoirs of American Folklore Society* 24:138–139 (1931)

    : Tales and Riddles Collected in Philadelphia, *Journal of American Folklore* 41:536–537, 544, 549–550 (1928)

: Negro Folk Tales from the South, *Journal of American Folklore* 40:259 (1927)

Majel Fritz: Death in the Graveyard, *New Mexico Folklore Record* 7:23–24 (1952–1953)

Lady Alice B. Gomme: *Traditional Games of England, Scotland, and Ireland,* 2 vols., David Nutt, London, 1894, 1898

Gumbo Ya-Ya. A Collection of Louisiana Folk Tales by Lyle Saxon, Robert Tallant, and Edward Dreyer, Houghton Mifflin Company, Boston, 1945

John Harland and T. T. Wilkinson: *Lancashire Folk-Lore,* Frederick Warne & Company, London, 1867, pp. 49–61

Melville J. and Frances S. Herskovits: *Suriname Folk-Lore,* Columbia University Press, New York, 1936

William Hone: *Table Book,* London, 1828

Zora Neale Hurston: *Mules and Men,* J. B. Lippincott Company, Philadelphia, 1935

Marcia Klein: Death in the Graveyard, *New Mexico Folklore Record* 6:27 (1951–1952)

Maria Leach: *Rainbow Book of American Folk Tales and Legends,* World Publishing Co., New York, 1958

: Personal archives of folklore and linguistics

Maria Leach and Jerome Fried: *Standard Dictionary of Folklore, Mythology, and Legend,* 2 vols., Funk & Wagnalls Company, New York, 1949–1950. Articles: *candle,* 186a; *elder,* 342c; *light,* 620a; *tongue twisters,* 1117cd

J. Alden Mason and Aurelio M. Espinosa: Porto Rican Folklore: Folktales, *Journal of American Folklore* 40:313–414 (1927)

E. Otero: Death in the Church, *New Mexico Folklore Record* 7:23 (1952–1953)

Elsie Clews Parsons: Folklore from the Cape Verde Islands, *Memoirs of American Folklore Society* 15:1:134–136 (1923)

Leonard Roberts: *South from Hell-fer-Sartin,* University of Kentucky Press, Lexington, 1955

Roland Steiner: Superstitions from Central Georgia, *Journal of American Folklore* 12:261–271 (1899)

Yoshimatsu Suzuki: *Japanese Legends and Folk-Tales,* Tokyo, 1951

Stith Thompson: *Motif-Index of Folk Literature,* 2d ed., 6 vols., Indiana University Press, Bloomington, 1955–1958

Stith Thompson and Jonas Balys: *Motif and Type Index of the Oral Tales of India,* Indiana University Press, Bloomington, 1958

ABOUT THE AUTHOR

MARIA LEACH is probably best known as compiler-editor of the distinguished two-volume *Standard Dictionary of Folklore, Mythology, and Legend*—the product of more than twelve years' research. American folklore has long been a special interest of hers, particularly in the areas of dialects, folk speech, and slang, and her love of the subject led to the writing of *The Rainbow Book of American Folk Tales and Legends*. In 1952 Mrs. Leach published her first book for children. Two years later came *The Soup Stone: The Magic of Familiar Things* and in 1956, *The Beginning: Creation Myths around the World*, for older readers. *God Had a Dog: The Folklore of the Dog* is her most recent book for adults.